Dragon's Hoard
NomNoms Vol. 1

edited by
Dreamous

**ADULT
READERS
ONLY**

DRAGON'S HOARD:
NOMNOMS VOLUME 1

Copyright © 2012
by Rabbit Valley
All rights reserved

Published by
Rabbit Valley Comics
Flagstaff, Arizona
https://www.rabbitvalley.com

ISBN 978-1-62475-018-2

Printed in the United States,
United Kingdom, or Australia
First printing January 2012
Second printing January 2022

Cover art by DarkNatasha
Interior art by Necrodrone,
Slate, DarkNatasha, Slug, and
Skulldog

Table of Contents

Front Cover by DarkNatasha

Insatiable

STORY by Mercy
ART by NecroDrone13

6

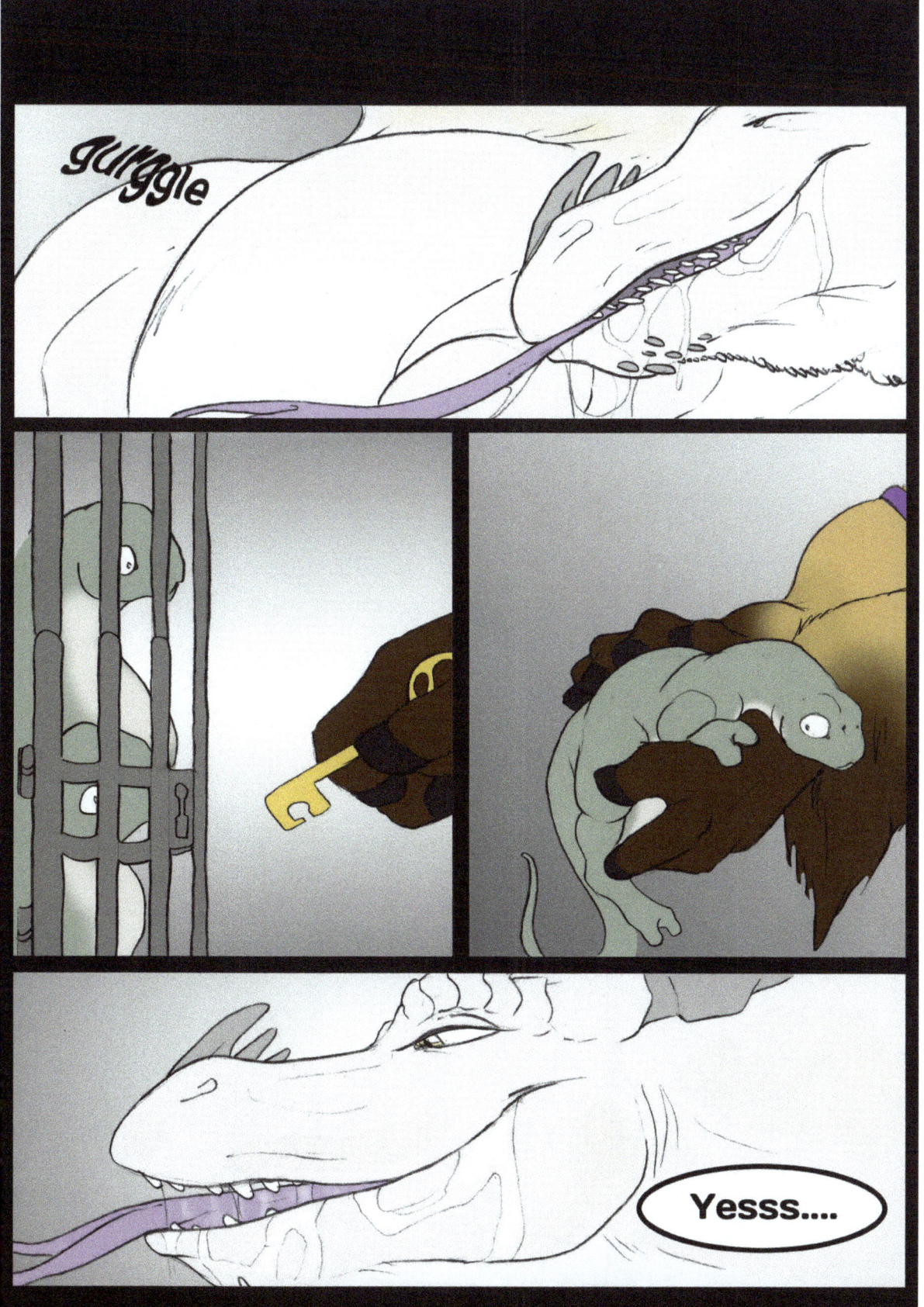

READERS DIGEST
BY SLATE

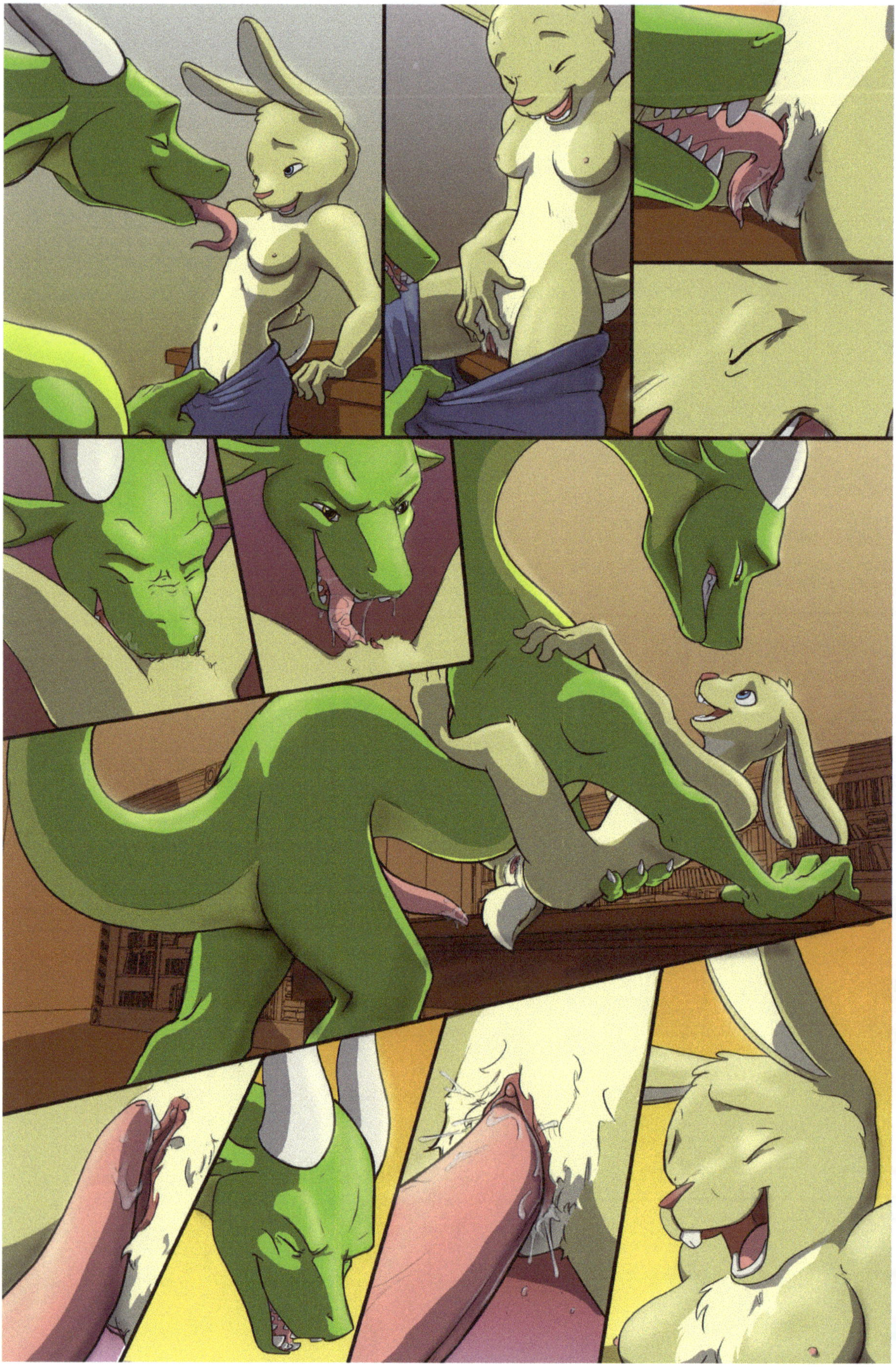

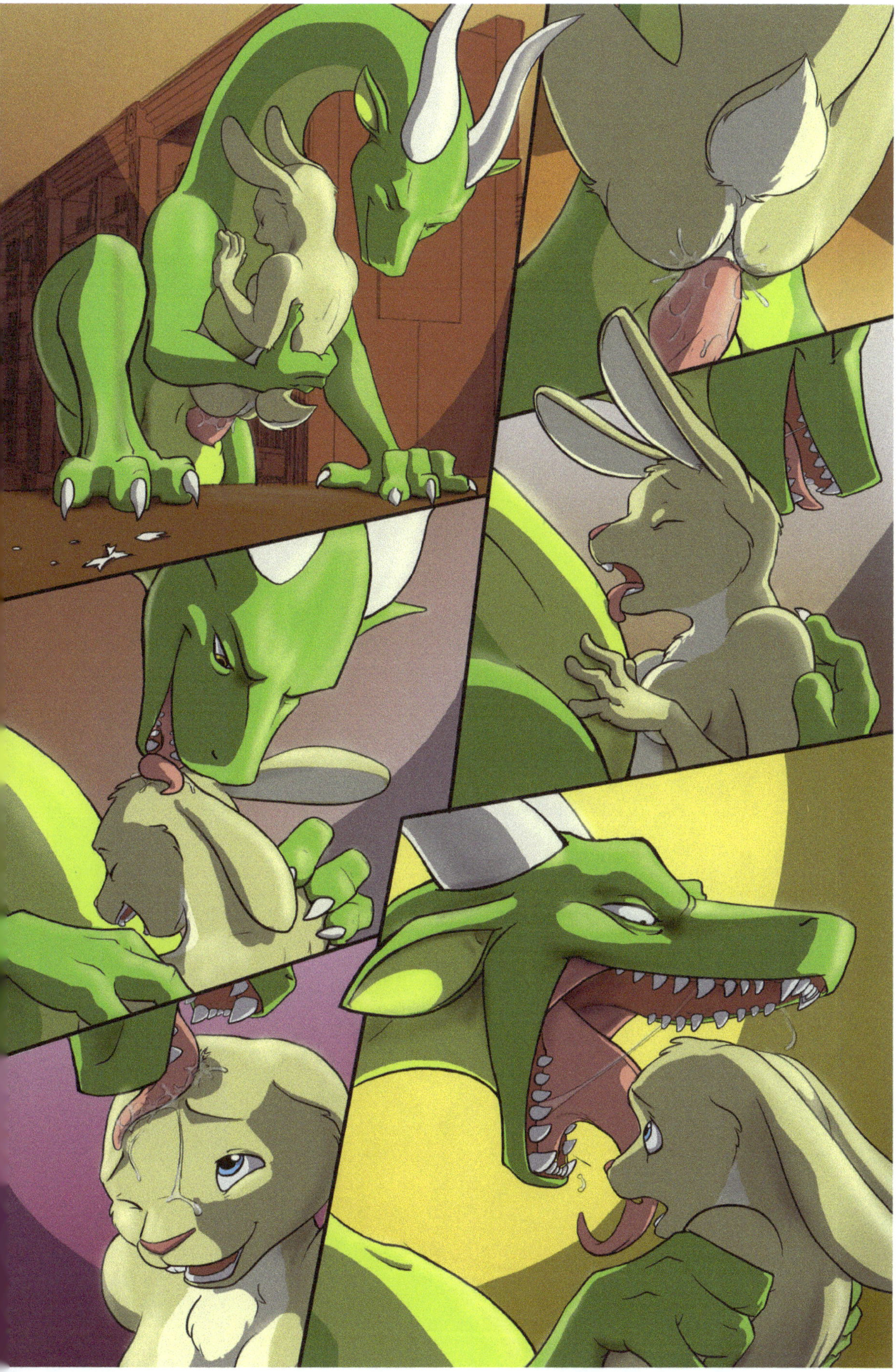

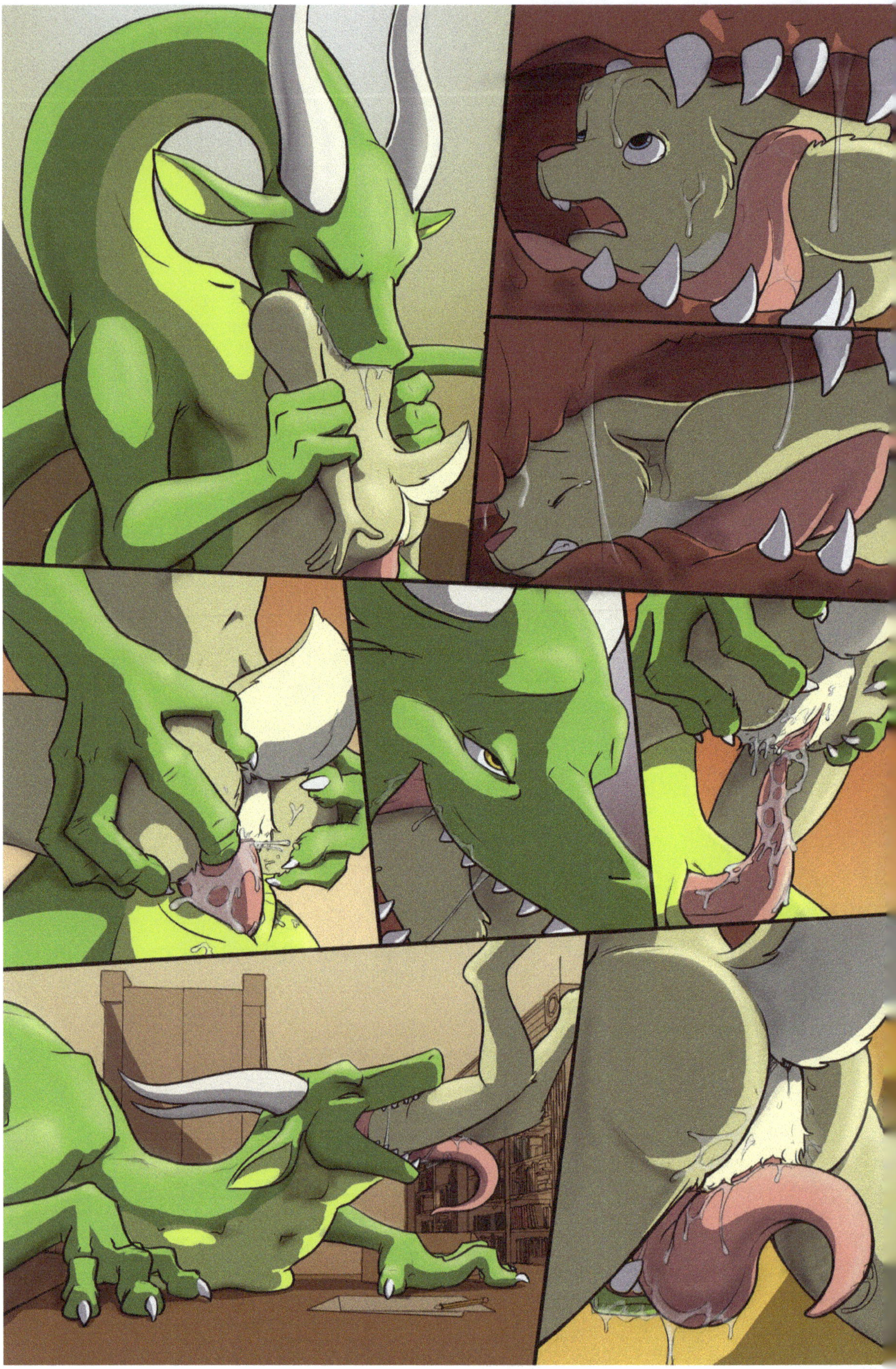

THE END

FOR WHOM THE BELL TOLLS

BY SLUG

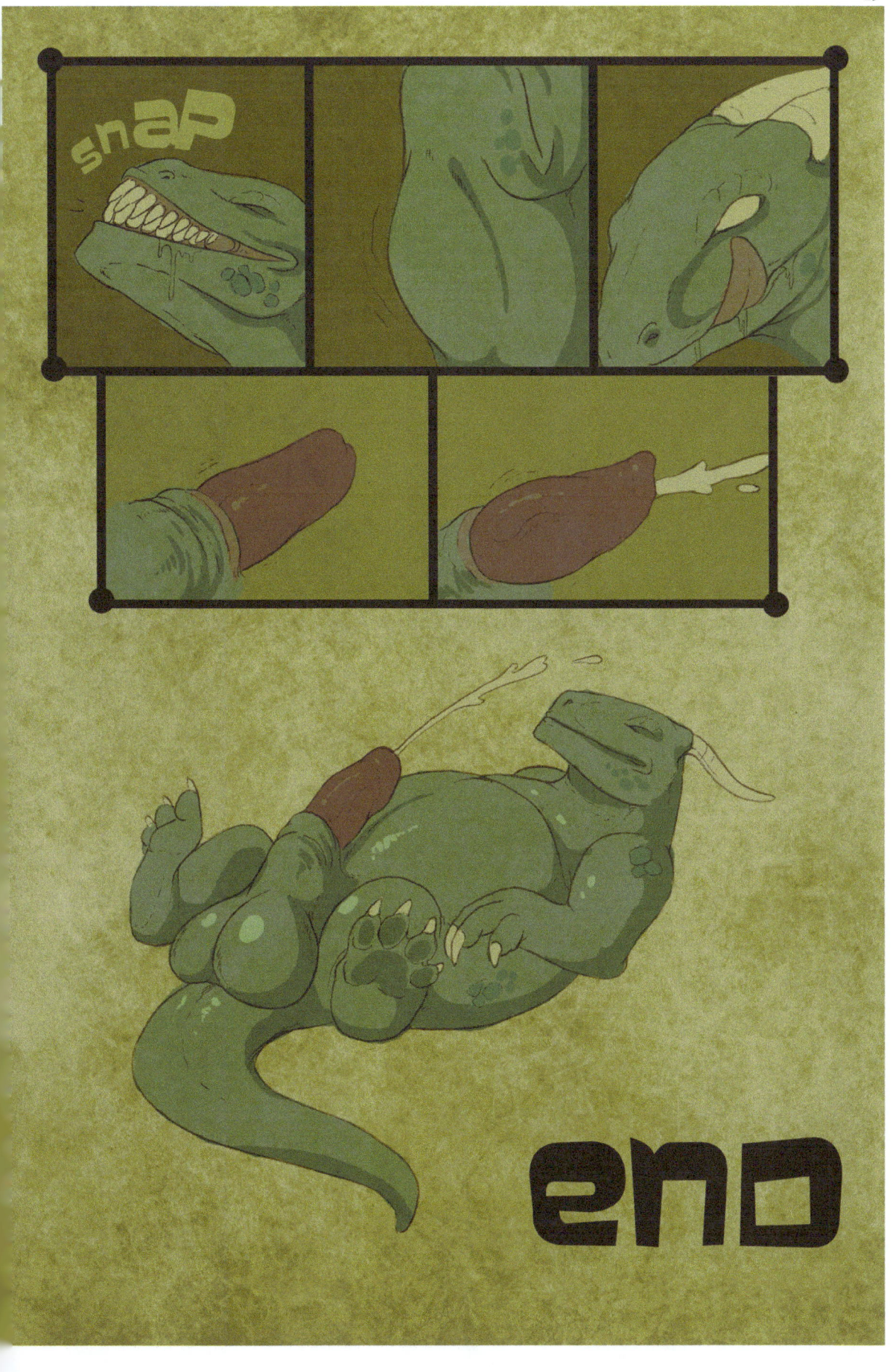

GRRR

I require.. assistance..

You there, the master calls! Go, go!

YAWN

THUD

But I!--

You'll do fine..

GRUMBLE

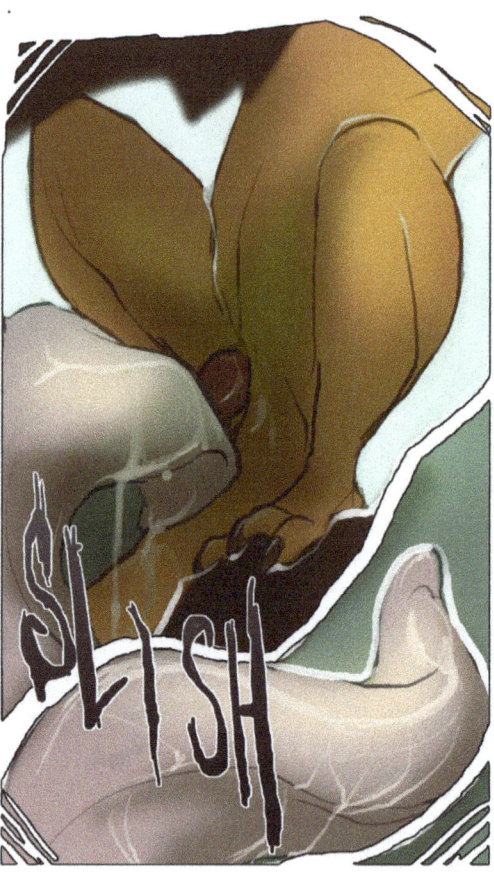

A note from **Spire**:

To my fellow ravenous dragons and ravenous dragon fans,

I cannot thank you enough for purchasing our comic. The continued support of so many dragons and dragon lovers has kept the Dragon's Hoard title going strong. I couldn't be happier continuing to help sate the seemingly unquenchable needs of our fans (though, hopefully, these little snacks have helped!).

I would like to add special thanks to the artists that have contributed, those who have helped me get the Dragon's Hoard name spread, those who helped gather material and, of course, our ever loving Dragon Valley... er, Rabbit Valley publisher. Without all of you this could not be possible, and I thank you from the bottom of my heart (or gut, or possibly more enjoyable lower regions).

If you enjoyed the comic, or if you want to contribute to the many Dragon's Hoard titles that are going to come out, or simply want to give your thoughts on the material contained within, please email me at dragonshoardcomic@gmail.com. I love you hear from the fans and your thoughts on what should be made next. Hearing your hopes and desires helps me shape what will be in future comics. Your ideas might even start a whole new comic series!

It really is all your enthusiam for these comics that keeps this old dragon wanting to do more, and I plan to! I hope you will all look forward to upcoming titles, many of which will be released at Further Confusion 2013. I hope to see you there!

If you like **Dragon's Hoard Presents: NomNoms**, please check out our other titles!

Dragon's Hoard Volumes 1 & 2 - Dragons upon dragons upon more dragons, and did I mention dragons? Nothing but classic feral dragon relations to sate the inner dragon in all of us!
Featured: feral on feral, feral on anthro, multiple gender pairings

Dragon's Hoard Presents: Runt - A comic by NecroDrone exploring the biology and social interactions of a feral dragon race. The comic focuses upon a Runt and his interactions with his loving peers.
Features: size play, dominance and submission, multiple fetishes, multiple genders

~Coming Soon~

Dragon's Hoard Presents: D.W.A.G.S. - A compilation comic featuring **D**ragons **W**ho **A**dvocate **G**ryphon **S**ubmission, one of the most basal (and personal favorite, for this dragon!) desires amongst our community- that sacred bond of dragon on gryphon love.
Features: feral dragon on gryphons, multiple genders

Dragon's Hoard Presents: Sacrifice - A comic by Spelunker Sal depicting the relationship between a dragon and the sacrifice that has been given to him.
Featured: feral dragon on anthro hare, male on male

Dragon's Hoard Volume 3 - The third installment of Dragon's Hoard, promising to bring yet more of our favorite king of love: the scaley kind! Come find us at FC to see what treasure we uncover.
Featured: feral on feral, feral on anthro, multiple genders

Sincerely and Lovingly,

(THE EVER HORNY)

DragonsHoardComic@gmail.com
www.furaffinity.net/user/dragonshoard